Good Days Bad Days

For Alison and Nick

ORCHARD BOOKS
96 Leonard Street, London EC2A 4XD
Orchard Books Australia
32/45-51 Huntley Street, Alexandria, NSW 2015
First published in Great Britain in 1990
This edition published in 2004
ISBN 1 84362 584 9
Text © Laurence Anholt 1990
Illustrations © Catherine Anholt 1990
The rights of Laurence Anholt to be identified as the author
and of Catherine Anholt to be identified as the illustrator
of this work has been asserted by them in accordance
with the Copyright, Designs and Patents Act 1988.
A CIP catalogue record for this book is available from the British Library.
10 9 8 7 6 5 4 3 2 1
Printed in Singapore

Good Days Bad Days

Catherine and Laurence Anholt

ORCHARD BOOKS

In our
family

we have

good days

bad days

happy days

sad days

work days

play days

home days

away days

sunny days

snowy days

rainy days

blowy days

healthy days

sick days

slow days

quick days

school days

Sundays

dull days

fun days.

Every day's a different day

but the best day follows yesterday . . .

TODAY!